Along Came Spider

JAMES PRELLER

SCHOLASTIC INC.

NEW YORK   TORONTO   LONDON   AUCKLAND   SYDNEY
MEXICO CITY   NEW DELHI   HONG KONG   BUENOS AIRES

Library of Congress Cataloging-in-Publication Data available on request.

ISBN-13: 978-0-545-03299-5
ISBN-10: 0-545-03299-7

12 11 10 9 8 7 6 5 4 3 2 1   8 9 10 11 12 13/0

Printed in the U.S.A.   40
First printing, September 2008

For all the evens, and the odds.

—JP

Along Came Spider

Along Came Spider

CONTENTS

CHAPTER ONE

Spider

Spider Stevens had a slight, lightweight body with long slender arms and spindly legs. From an early age, Robert (the name given to him at birth) was a natural climber. He earned his nickname during gym class due to his skill at the climbing wall. "Holy jeez," whistled Mr. Z, the gym teacher. "You zip up that wall like a spider." So the dull birth name was packed in mothballs and "Spider" Stevens was born — like a butterfly emerging from a chrysalis, but way cooler than that.

Spider's neighborhood friend, Trey Cooper, could never quite get used to the new nickname.

"Hey Robert, are you coming over after school

today?" Trey asked, as they hung their jackets in their cubbies.

Spider rolled his eyes. Trey always got it wrong. "You know everybody calls me Spider now."

"Oh right," Trey said with a quick nod. "Like the poem with Miss Muffet."

Spider just groaned...but he couldn't get mad at Trey.

Now he sat in room 511 and stared hopelessly at a page of his writing journal. The page, like his mind at the moment, was blank. Spider fiddled with his pencil, scratched his nose, and looked around. At Spiro Agnew Elementary, Spider and his fifth-grade classmates were at the top of the food chain. Middle school would come the following year, complete with gum-jammed lockers, endless hallways, and untold dangers. But at Agnew Elementary, fifth graders were like lions on the savanna.

On this morning Spider had already survived a math lesson—multiplying fractions, ugh—and was halfway into reading and language arts. Mrs.

Wine set aside time each day for her students to pull out their writing folders and Think Deep Thoughts. Meanwhile, she met briefly one-on-one with students at the back table. The meetings didn't last long, but they always filled Spider with dread. He had to sit directly across from his teacher with all his thoughts laid out like an open book — *exactly* like an open book.

Overall, Spider liked fifth grade. Teachers didn't treat them like little kids anymore. Because — duh — they weren't. Most of all, he enjoyed the freedom. So in a totally weird way, Spider preferred Writer's Workshop over any other time of the school day (except for, it goes without saying, the Big Three: P.E., lunch, and recess).

And once you subtracted the face-to-face-with-the-teacher part of it, Writer's Workshop was Not Bad. Not Bad equals Pretty Good, if you turn it upside down and squint. Except that Spider couldn't think of anything to put on paper. Mrs. Wine insisted that it could be "anything you want! The world is your oyster!" (Spider had no idea what that meant, except that he didn't like oysters and had no intention of eating one, ever: Way Too Gross Looking.)

To Spider, the idea of writing about *anything* was…insane. Where would he start? Open a dictionary and pick a path from aardvark to zucchini? He could write about motorbikes or basketball or the everyday weirdness of living with his grandmother, an old lady who loved watching her soaps on television every afternoon. She was a total loon and Spider loved her. Should he write about that? Some things—maybe even *most* things—were better left unsaid. Or in this case, unwritten.

But that still left the blank page in Spider's journal. He'd have to fill it with *something*. Even if he wrote extra large, with plenty of space between the words, it wouldn't be easy. How could he reduce "anything" to Any One Thing?

Where do ideas come from, anyway? mused Spider. He almost laughed when he thought of it: *from stores like Wal-Mart and Home Depot. Why not? They have everything else!* Spider wished that he could pick up a few ideas in aisle 7B, right between "plumbing" and "wall fixtures." He imagined himself stepping up to the counter with an armload of items. He'd say to the bored cashier, "Yeah, let's see, I'll have this stuff, a box of Junior Mints, and any ideas you might have lying around out back. I have to do this writer's journal in school, and, well…I ran out of ideas."

Spider glanced around the room, hoping to find an idea.

Blaaaattt, ker-HONK!

No, that wasn't a flock of geese flying overhead (though it was mid-October and high time to head south). The snarfling sounds came from the perpetually congested Joseph Waters up in the front row. Joseph always had a runny nose. All day long he provided a soggy soundtrack for what was supposed to be Quiet Time: *Kerffle, snurrffle, snort!* It was like somebody appointed Joseph boss of Truly Gross Sounds.

Next to Joseph sat the kid in shorts, Satchel

Lewis. He took pride in being the first boy in shorts after winter and the last kid in pants in the fall. He basically wore shorts unless it was, like, twenty degrees below and windy. As an added bonus, one of Satchel's sneakers (specifically, the left one) was always untied.

Spider could hear Mrs. Wine finishing up with Ava Bright. Ava was new to the school, having moved to town from, um, Somewhere Else. Ava seemed to be fitting in okay enough, though it was obvious that she was Not From Here. For starters, she wore those clunky glasses. In Spider's suburban town, if you wanted to fit in, it was best to be like everybody else.

For better or for worse, Spider noted, Ava was different in most ways. She was fascinated by survival handbooks, which made her good to have around in case of trouble. Let's say Spider wanted to know how to proceed if he were attacked by 1) a bear; or 2) a swarm of bees. Ava Bright would be able to provide quick, practical advice: 1) Play dead and hope; and 2) Don't swat, just run away.

She knew how to survive in a desert, how to keep safe during a tornado, and how to land a plane in case of…whatever.

Spider glanced at the wall clock. He checked the day's schedule to kill some time. Next stop: the library, then snack, then geography. It was all on the blackboard, the whole day planned down to the millisecond. Spider leaned back and closed his eyes. An unwelcome smell hit his nostrils.

It could mean only one thing: Howie Stone. Sometime over the summer Howie discovered cologne. He slathered it on by the gallon. Thanks to Howie, room 511 smelled like a fruit cup that had been left out too long in the sun.

Spider scribbled in his journal:

Howie Stone is like that skunk from the cartoons—Pepé Le Pew!

He sketched a little picture to go with it, drawing Howie as a cartoon character with wriggly lines rising up all around him. Nice. He turned the page and drew a sketch of Ava Bright falling off a cliff, her nose buried in a thick book titled *When Bad Things Happen to Good People.*

At last, Spider had something to write about in his journal. The kids of room 511 — in graphic novel form! If Mrs. Wine wanted "anything," then Spider would give it to her. The classroom overflowed with characters. But there was no one more interesting than Trey Cooper. Spider glanced back and to his right, and there was Trey, lining up a tidy row of pencils, humming tune-lessly to himself, lost in space.

Trey lived on 19 Maple Street, within easy walking distance of Agnew Elementary. The house to the right of Trey's, 21 Maple, was where Spider grew up. They lived, obviously, on the odd side of the street — which seemed about right.

CHAPTER TWO

Trey

Trey Cooper was hard at work, studying the four walls of room 511. There were posters everywhere he looked. While there were fancy maps from *National Geographic*, most of the posters were handmade. And Trey felt sure that the hands that made the posters were attached to the arms of Mrs. Wine.

There were posters labeled "Class Birthdays," "Guidelines for Writer's Workshops," or "Books We Shared." Each poster featured a variety of different marker colors, on the (correct) assumption that students would grow bored reading a single color. Trey imagined Mrs. Wine at home, a large white poster on a table, a box of colored markers at her side. First she would draw a blue sentence, then green, then red. Trey imagined her set of markers in a perfect line, the colors aligned to follow the pattern of the spectrum: red, orange, yellow, green, blue, and violet. Neat and sweet.

Trey's favorite poster looked like this:

CREATING SMILES
Say Something Nice to Someone
☺

You Look Nice • Hello! •
Thanks for Your Help • Way to Go! •
A-OK • Bravo! • Well Done • You
Are Awesome • Keep Up the Good
Work • You Rock • I Know You Can
Do It • How Are You? • Super •
You're the Best • Cool!

Trey read the poster several times each day, carefully memorizing the phrases. He liked the idea — how one simple remark could twist a face into a smile. It seemed like magic, a bag of tricks he could use to create happiness. Trey repeated the lines to himself: *Well done! You rock! Keep up the good work! Thanks for your help!*

Easy-cheesy.

Mrs. Wine had moved to the front of the room and was now talking about something or other. Trey realized that Writer's Workshop was officially over. He also sensed Mrs. Mowatt, the classroom aide, hovering somewhere behind him, like a balloon in the Macy's Thanksgiving Day Parade. She was large and overflowing and smelled of cocoa butter. Trey liked her, though Mrs. Mowatt was always reminding him to write down the homework assignment, put away his folders, neaten his desk, stop twirling his ruler, pay attention, and on and on. She was sort of like a very large gnat.

Trey had one ear open to hear Mrs. Wine's instructions, the other tuned to the inner rumble of his own brain. There were times when Trey's mind kind of clouded over, like a rainy afternoon. He could hear his teacher's voice, but he couldn't always connect to the words that swam like fish in the air. Instead, Trey floated, floated up and out the window, high into the clouds, beyond the sun, into the...

"Trey, *pssst,* Trey!"

A voice came from nearby, insistent. It was Olive Desmond, the skinny black-haired girl who sat next to Trey. She was staring at him.

Trey, in turn, stared at the green ribbon she used to tie her hair back in a ponytail. It wasn't dark green and it wasn't exactly light green, either. Trey thought of his old, battered set of crayons at home—the huge 128-color box—and wondered where in that box he'd place the color of Olive's green ribbon. He decided that it would slip in nicely between the Sea Green and Spring Green crayons. Some people thought Trey was too old to like crayons, but Trey knew that some people were wrong.

Olive Desmond hissed at him. *Hisssst.* She sounded like a flat tire.

"What?"

"You were making that noise again." She shook her head and the green ribbon bounced.

Trey shrugged. "So?"

"It's annoying," Olive stated matter-of-factly.

Trey nodded, still humming softly, *hum-dee-dum, dee-dum-dum*. He patiently waited for Olive to stop looking at him, stop rolling her eyes, stop holding her mouth in that funny way of hers.

And at that moment Trey decided that his pencils really, really needed sharpening.

Trey Cooper was particular about his pencils. He liked them sharpened to a perfect point, like a warrior's spear. No matter what was happening at the moment, if Trey broke a pencil tip, or noticed that his supply of perfectly pointed pencils was running low, or simply felt an urge to move around, Trey had to respond—immediately, ASAP, pronto. Like: now. In the hierarchy of human needs, along with food, water, and shelter, for Trey there was a fourth necessity: sharpened pencils.

Trey obeyed the impulse and made his way to the pencil sharpener on the ledge beside the windows. Oh, the satisfaction it gave him to push in that broken point, turn the handle, and feel the vibration in his fingers as it shaved thin slivers of wood. Trey twirled the handle and gazed out the wall-length windows to the playground outside.

Trey wasn't sure when, exactly, the room fell silent. It might have been 10:47 or 10:49 or sometime in between. Trey was humming along as he honed his third pencil to a fine point when something—a stillness—caused him to look up from his task. Everyone was staring.

Mrs. Wine was looking intently at him, hands on her hips, lips tight, like she was sucking on a Sour Patch Kid. The tips of her ears had gone bright red. Three rhyming words—hips, lips, and tips—all signaled Mrs. Wine's unhappiness. Trey was getting better at figuring these things out. *Hips, lips, tips. Hips, lips, tips.*

"Are you finished?" she asked.

Trey thought for a moment, considering Mrs.

Wine's question. He decided that it was a trick question, one that he had better not answer (since, of course — obviously! — he was not finished, nowhere close, for he still had seven pencils to go). At the same time, she expected a response of some kind. Mrs. Wine stood looking at him, that sour expression still on her face, waiting for something.

Thinking of the poster, Trey blurted, "A-OK!"

"Excuse me?"

"Super!" Trey exclaimed, beaming.

"Please take your seat, Trey. We'll discuss this later."

"Mrs. Wine," Trey answered, "you are awesome...and you rock!"

Strange, Trey thought as he made his way back to his seat. *Mrs. Wine didn't smile back.*

Something must be wrong with that poster.

CHAPTER THREE

Hoops for Heart

"All righty, let's get started," Mrs. Wine greeted her groggy students the next morning. She gestured to the blackboard (which was, Spider noted, *green*). "You should be writing down tonight's homework assignment. Meanwhile, folders should be out and papers turned in."

After the pledge and morning announcements, Mrs. Wine reminded the class about the annual "Hoops for Heart" program.

"As you know, all of the money we raise goes to the American Heart Association," she explained. "Last year we raised enough money to rank first among schools our size in the state of New York."

A whoop of cheers rose up and sailed out the open windows. Mrs. Wine smiled. "You deserve that applause," she said. "I'd like to remind you of a few things before we begin our day. Most important, everyone can participate in this program. You don't have to be a basketball star like…um, er, like…"

Her face went blank. "Okay, who can name a basketball star for me? Sports aren't my strong suit."

A bunch of kids called out names of favorite players: "Dwayne Wade!" "Kevin Garnett!" "Carmelo Anthony!"

"Fine, fine, that's enough, thank you," Mrs. Wine said, laughing at the enthusiastic response. "You'll need to continue to get pledges from your family and neighbors. They are due next week."

"I got enough pledges last year to earn a free basketball," Cissy Apunama announced.

"I got a pump rocket launcher," Justin Seo said,

"but this year I want to get enough pledges for a digital camera."

"This pledge drive isn't supposed to bring on a case of the gimme-gimme-gimmes," Mrs. Wine reminded the class, raising her eyebrows. "On the weekend of the 24th, we'll have skills stations, foul shooting, dribbling, and whatever else it is that you basketball players do, all for a good cause."

"There's the tournament, too," Ryan Donovan reminded Mrs. Wine.

"That's right," she said. "There will be a friendly three-on-three basketball tournament for students in grades four and five. As I understand it, even teachers are allowed to play."

"Oh, do it, do it, Mrs. Wine!" Spider exclaimed. He grinned at the thought of Mrs. Wine in gym shorts and sneakers. She didn't look the type. Spider remembered the first time he saw one of his teachers out in the real world. It was his first-grade teacher, Mrs. Frick, at the supermarket. She was squeezing a grapefruit. It seemed So Totally Wrong to Spider.

A chorus of voices joined in with Spider, all advising their teacher to sign up for the tournament. Mrs. Wine held up both hands and shook her head. "Two words," she said. "No. Way."

"Awww, boo!" roared Ryan Donovan. Everybody laughed at the thought of Mrs. Wine chucking up air balls from all over the court.

Mrs. Wine waved away the catcalls, smiling. "Okay, that's enough, boys and girls. As I've told you before, basketball is not my sport. But if there's ever an ice-cream-eating contest, I'll be the first to sign up."

Trey Cooper's hand rocketed skyward. He had something urgent to say, rightthisminute, and it couldn't wait. "Did you know, Mrs. Wine, that air is one of the most important ingredients in ice cream?" Trey blurted. "Without air, ice cream would be as hard as a brick wall!"

"That's very interesting, Trey," Mrs. Wine noted. "But right now I'd like to —"

"The world's biggest ice cream sundae was made in Alberta, Canada!" Trey announced, barely pausing to breathe. "It was built in 1988 and weighed almost 55,000 pounds!"

The class sat in silence, though they weren't surprised. They knew Trey did this kind of thing all the time. He would periodically call out random facts, such as: "Polar bears are left-handed!" (Which was supposedly true, though how scientists figured that out Spider could not imagine. A quick game of Ping-Pong?) It didn't bother Trey that nobody seemed interested. It was as if he experienced a buildup of pressure and needed to release the tension into the stratosphere, like steam coming from a teakettle. The kettle whistled; it didn't particularly care if anyone whistled back.

Because of just this sort of thing, by the time Trey had reached fifth grade, pretty much all the kids in Agnew Elementary had noticed that he was a little *off*. They used different words for it. Some words strained to be nice, others didn't:

peculiar, different, quirky, unusual, loser, odd-ball, strange, freak.

It was hard to pin down exactly what was wrong with Trey. No, not *wrong*. It was more an issue of his extreme "not-normalness." Mostly it was a bunch of little things, Trey's bag of quirks that gave rise to the general conclusion: "Trey Cooper is Out There."

Or in the words of Howie Stone, "mad weird."

Trey had been labeled "the oddball" long ago. Maybe now that's all anybody could see, the label and not the boy. After a while — third grade, fourth grade, fifth grade — nobody except for Spider bothered to figure Trey out anymore.

Trey was tolerated and ignored.

"Thank you, Trey," Mrs. Wine said. "Those are very interesting facts about ice cream." She glanced hopefully around the classroom. "Does anyone else have a *question* about Hoops for Heart?"

Ava Bright tentatively raised her hand. "Mrs. Wine, what if someone can't find a team?"

"Good question, Ava," Mrs. Wine replied, relieved to get back on the subject. "If anyone needs help finding team members, please note it on your permission slip and I will help you."

She looked at Ava, who still seemed doubtful. "Okay?"

Ava nodded, brown hair parted to the side, cascading over her thick-framed glasses.

"Oh, look at the time," Mrs. Wine exclaimed. "Let's pull out our social studies texts and turn to page thirty-seven."

The morning went on as usual. No more weird outbursts from Trey. The class was filing outside for a quick break when Ryan Donovan caught up with Spider.

Ryan was tall and thick-bodied, with short-cropped hair and wide shoulders. He jerked his head in the direction of Trey, who trailed behind the others. Ryan asked Spider, "I don't get it. How come you're friends with that kid?"

Spider shrugged. "He's my next-door neighbor. We grew up together."

"So, big deal," Ryan said. "It doesn't mean you have to hang out with him."

Spider cast a backward glance at Trey, who was fumbling for something inside his desk. Mrs. Mowatt, the classroom aide, was standing beside him. Trey's shirt was untucked and his hair looked like a bird's nest.

"Trey isn't bad once you get to know him," Spider tried to explain. "He's a little weird sometimes, but..."

"A *little* weird?" Ryan echoed. "Try, like, majorly weird—*all* the time. Look, if you want to hang out with him, that's your business." His message was clear. If Spider kept hanging out with Trey, it wasn't going to win him any points with Ryan and his friends.

Kurt Hull joined the conversation, dressed as usual in a sports jersey. Kurt didn't seem to own a shirt without a team logo plastered across it. "We're playing basketball at recess after lunch today. Are you guys in?"

"You know it," Ryan answered.

"Yeah, that'd be cool," Spider said.

"So far it's us three, plus Billy and Justin. We'll need a couple more for four-on-four," Kurt said, as he squished his boot in a patch of mud.

"Hey, maybe we could team up for the tournament," Ryan suggested. "I can play D and rebound. Kurt can score. And Spider, you can be our point guard. We'd be unbeatable."

"Really?" Spider asked. "You want me?" Spider knew he was a good player, he just hadn't realized that anybody else had noticed.

"Yeah, you're one of the best dribblers in school," Ryan said. "Your crossover is mad quick."

"And you actually pass the ball," Kurt chimed in. "Not like some ball hogs we know."

Ryan gave Kurt a fist-tap. "Us three," he said. "We can win the whole thing."

"I don't know if the tournament works like that," Spider countered. "Mrs. Wine said they don't even keep score."

Ryan frowned. "She doesn't know anything about sports."

"Yeah, but…"

"We'll definitely keep score," Kurt quickly said. "There's no point playing if you don't keep score." The very idea seemed to offend him.

"Yeah, I guess," Spider replied. He didn't want to argue. Besides, it felt good to be included with Ryan and Kurt. The three of them would make an awesome team. Spider had known Ryan and Kurt for a long time, but this was the first year they had all been in the same class. It felt like something big had just happened. A shift.

Spider had been drafted onto the "A" team.

CHAPTER FOUR

Wolves

The way Trey Cooper saw it, most of the boys in school were like wolves — and recess was when they roamed free. Those same boys who sat in orderly rows under the watchful eyes of Mrs. Wine, the boys who politely raised their hands and called out answers, the boys who filed away schoolbooks and lined up for library? They all changed when the doors flung open. *Like wolves,* Trey thought. Their snouts grew long, and their teeth turned sharp and dangerous.

Wolves traveled in packs. And Trey did not belong. So he watched them from a safe distance. Trey felt separate and alone, and that was okay.

He could live with it. But sometimes Trey wondered what it might be like to run with the pack.

Certain parts of the school day — like lunchtime and recess — were harder for Trey. Often he wandered around on the edges, drifting like a cloud, counting his steps, aimless. Trey never liked rushing from one thing to the next. Mrs. Mowatt once tried to explain it to him. She said that Trey had a tough time with "transitions." If that meant he wasn't crazy about recess, Trey agreed.

He liked the outdoors, though, the wide-openness; so Trey killed time by wandering around the rectangular basketball court. His friend Spider was playing, and Trey liked that. He always rooted for Spider, wishing the ball into the hoop every time Spider hoisted up a shot. Trey watched now as a loose cluster of boys, joined by the Papadopoulos twins, Leah and Lacey, took warm-up shots on the basketball court.

Thwap, thwappita, thwappp. The game had its own music. It was like a drumbeat, a heartbeat, and Spider controlled the rhythm with the force and speed of each bounce. *Thwap, thwappp, thwap-thwap-thwap.* Spider dribbled the ball effortlessly: behind his back, between his legs, right hand, left hand. The ball on his fingertips became like an extension of his brain, a yo-yo on an invisible string. Spider let the ball go in a high, lazy rainbow. *Swish,* it shivered through the metal net.

"All right, let's pick teams," Kurt announced. "Who are the captains?"

Divided into two teams, four on each side, they began the game. Spider teamed up with Ryan, Justin Seo, and Leah Papadopoulos. They went up against Kurt, Billy Timmons, Joseph Waters, and Leah's fraternal twin, Lacey.

It wasn't hard to tell the twins apart. Leah — the older Papadopoulos by three minutes — was taller and had dark hair. Lacey's hair was blond and she had sky-blue eyes. Trey didn't understand how they could be twins at all, since looking the same was clearly the most important part of being a twin. Otherwise, why bother? But one thing was certain: Those Papadopoulos girls sure could play. Better than most boys, though no one liked to admit it.

Walking around and around, sometimes stopping to pick up a rock or move a stick, Trey watched the game out of the corners of his eyes. He was looking like he was not looking, a little trick he had learned. He liked things that way. Trey couldn't explain it, but sometimes an open stare hurt, made his skin crawl. So he often looked down, or to the side, and watched the world that way.

Like always, the game was hard-fought and physical. Play had been getting rougher as autumn deepened, much to the displeasure of Mrs. Jenkins, the noon aide. The Papadopoulos twins traded baskets, Ryan rebounded like a maniac, and Spider controlled the tempo with his dribbling and passing. With the score tied at 7–7, Justin emerged from a knot of players, clutching an injured finger.

"Ow, I jammed it!" Justin whimpered. "I'm done, guys."

The game stopped cold. "We need another player," Ryan said, scanning the area for a fill-in.

"I'll play," a voice bleated. Trey was surprised to discover it was his own voice that had spoken. It was as if he had wanted to play all along, but hadn't admitted it to himself. Trey didn't know what he felt until the words flew past his lips.

"No way," Ryan retorted. "He's awful."

"Why not?" Spider countered. "The game is almost over, anyway. We need a body."

Trey stood alone on the grass behind the basket. The boys argued over him as if he were invisible. But he heard every word. And the truth was, Ryan was right. Trey didn't know much about playing basketball. Sure, he knew that some guy named Kareem Abdul-Jabbar held the NBA record with 38,387 career points. He also knew that on March 2, 1962, Wilt Chamberlain scored one hundred points in a single game. But those were just numbers filed away in the back

31

of his brain. They weren't the game itself, the chaos of running around on the court like crazy chickens.

Trey could shoot a little bit if there was no one getting in his way. He specialized in behind-the-back trick shots, but had never been on a real team before. His parents never signed him up for the town league. Basketball games looked like a squirming mass of worms wriggling around without rhyme or reason. *But even so,* Trey figured, *so what? How hard could it be?*

If Wilt could score one hundred points, maybe Trey could manage two.

CHAPTER FIVE

Nose to Nose

On the court, Spider reasoned with Ryan. "It's just a game. Let's give him a chance." And without waiting for permission, Spider bounced a pass to Trey. "You're on our team. Game's to eleven, we're tied, seven up."

Trey's face brightened. "Like the soda! Seven-Up — cool and refreshing!"

"Oh, brother." Ryan grimaced, shaking his head.

Trey walked onto the court, grateful for the opportunity to play. But before the game even started again, he quickly called, "Time-out!" Trey went to the side of the court and emptied his pockets of about half a dozen rocks, which he lined neatly on the grass.

Watching Trey fumble around with his rocks while the others grumbled impatiently, Spider was hit with an instant wave of regret. It would have been so much easier to pick somebody else — *anybody* else.

What was I thinking? Spider wondered. *Why did I invite Trey to play basketball?* He could think of a hundred reasons why he shouldn't invite Trey. But he could think of only one reason why he should. Spider and Trey had a history together. They had been friends since…back in the day.

Spider and Trey were born six weeks apart and grew up next door to each other. And so the boys naturally became fast friends. For a long time, Trey was the only *real* friend Spider knew; he had no one else to compare him to, nothing to measure Trey against. So if he was in any way out of the ordinary, it was only a case of Trey being perfectly himself.

Take Trey's fascination with rocks. He could spend hours gathering and organizing his collection of stones. Trey lined them up outside in complex patterns, circling trees, forming mazes, totally engrossed in his designs.

There were times when Spider would wander over to play with Trey, but it was as if Trey had gone deaf and mute, the world fading to gray wallpaper. Spider learned to accept Trey during those times when he was alone in his own world. He would walk away, find something else to do. But sometimes it would be Incredibly Frustrating. Why wouldn't Trey answer?

When they were younger, Spider once got so mad he swung his foot and sent dozens of stones flying. Trey flipped out. He wasn't angry at Spider. It was much worse than that. Trey was crushed, as if his orderly world had been turned upside down. And there was nothing, no *thing*, that Spider could do to make it better. Only when Trey's mother came out the back door blowing bubbles from a small plastic wand did he finally settle down. Trey slumped to the ground, watching the bubbles float in the breeze, soothed and at peace. Spider never again touched Trey's stones.

So, okay, sure, that was a Little Weird. But for Spider it was just Trey being Trey.

It wasn't that Spider learned how to tolerate Trey or even "understand" him. It was more than that; Spider came to admire Trey. He watched Trey build things, deep in concentration as he labored over one of the many birdhouses he assembled. (Though, as Trey would insist, they were *technically* called nest boxes.) Trey was special; it didn't take a rocket scientist to figure it out. The truth was, in his younger days Spider loved Trey as much as any preschooler can love a friend — and that was a lot.

You don't turn your back on that.

Not easily, that's for sure.

And that was why he passed the ball to Trey Cooper. But in the span of two minutes, Trey's man, sneezy Joseph Waters, got open for two easy layups. It was all beginning to look like a big mistake.

"Come on, Trey!" Ryan said sharply. "D up!"

Trey looked at Ryan wonderingly. Spider could tell Trey was clueless.

"On defense, try to stay between Joseph and the basket," Spider advised. "Don't let him get behind you."

A minute later, on the other end of the court, Trey flubbed a perfect pass from Spider. The next time down the court, his shot was blocked by Kurt Hull. "Not in my house!" Kurt rejoiced, rising high and swatting the ball away.

All the while, Ryan Donovan fumed like a smoldering volcano. Spider could see it, *anyone* could see it—except for Trey Cooper, who seemed to think this was just a game and not a matter of life and death.

Trey wasn't very good at reading body language.

"Don't pass to him anymore," Ryan ordered Spider.

Spider wasn't about to let Ryan Donovan tell

him what to do. He replied by instantly threading a pass to Trey. The ball trickled between Trey's fingers and rolled out of bounds.

"See what I mean?" Ryan sneered. "We're going to lose because of him!"

Spider saw what Ryan meant. Heck, anybody could see that Trey was killing their team's chances of winning.

By freezing Trey out of the offense, never passing him the ball, and doubling up to guard Trey's man on defense, Spider's team managed to tie the game, 10 up.

"Next bucket wins," Billy announced.

Spider dribbled to the top of the key. Leah was covered tight by Lacey. Spider looked to pass to Ryan, but he couldn't get open. Kurt and Billy were on him too tight.

"I'm open! I'm open!" Trey called. He stood alone on the baseline. After all, there was no reason to guard Trey Cooper.

Spider's instinct took over. The ball left his fingertips before he had a chance to think. That's how the game was supposed to be played: You hit the open man, even if it's Trey Cooper.

Somehow Trey managed to catch the ball. All he had to do was sink a six-foot shot, and they'd win the game. He'd be the hero. But Trey dribbled *away* from the basket, retreating to the far corner of the court.

What is he up to now? Spider thought.

"Pass it!" Ryan demanded.

Leah cut to the corner. She clapped two hands, calling for the ball. "Kick it out, back to me," she called.

Suddenly Trey spun around, bounced the ball once, and kicked it high into the air. The ball sailed over the backboard and out of bounds.

Spider's heart sank like a stone. Trey blew the shot on purpose.

"What are you doing?" Ryan cried. He stormed toward Trey. "You're not even trying!"

Ryan's raised voice attracted the attention of Mrs. Jenkins, the noon aide. She was a no-nonsense woman, short and stout like a teapot.

Mrs. Jenkins turned and focused her eagle eyes on the basketball court.

"You're screwing up the whole game," Ryan complained.

"It's okay," Spider said, trying to calm down his teammate. He tugged on Ryan's sleeve. "Come on. Let's play defense. Just ignore him. We can still win." Spider looked at Trey and shook his head.

"What's wrong with you?" Ryan demanded, pulling away from Spider. The thick-necked boy lurched toward Trey and stood, fists clenched, staring into his eyes like an open threat.

CHAPTER SIX

The Wall

Trey had no answer. He just stood there, hands dangling at his sides, tongue-tied. He averted his eyes to the ground. *What was wrong with him?* "I'm okay," he softly declared. "How about you?"

"You think this is a joke?" Ryan asked. "I don't see what's so funny." He stepped closer to Trey, crowding him, forcing him to take a half step back.

Ryan was standing too close. Much too close. Trey felt tense, uncomfortable, trapped. He suddenly found it hard to breathe. Ryan was loud and his face was too near and his staring eyes hurt and his mouth smelled like garlic. Trey squeezed his eyes shut.

And pushed.

Ryan stumbled backward, surprised at the sudden ferocity of Trey's shove.

Bleeaat, bleeaatt! A shrill whistle blew. Up rushed Mrs. Jenkins in her periwinkle sweatsuit, pointing at the two boys.

"That's enough!" she commanded. "Game's over. No more basketball for the week."

"What?!" Kurt Hull cried. "No more —"

"Not another word," Mrs. Jenkins ordered. "Trey, Ryan, I want both of you against the wall for the remainder of recess. As for the rest of you, I advise that you find something else to do."

The wall was legendary. In the playground world, no one wanted to get sent to the wall. And for that very reason, the wall was the noon aide's favorite form of punishment. Once banished to the wall, a student had no choice but to stand by while everyone else ran free. The wall wasn't just punishment. It was torture.

Ryan leaned against the brick wall, glaring at Trey. "It's your fault," he grumbled.

"No talking, Mr. Donovan, unless you'd like to stand there all week," Mrs. Jenkins snapped. She seemed to be enjoying herself. That was why the boys called her "the Queen of Mean."

Trey may have been the only person at Agnew Elementary who didn't actually mind standing at the wall. In truth, it was kind of nice. The wall came as a relief, a break from playground life. Now Trey knew exactly where to go and what to do. There was no more confusion, no more decisions to make.

Unlike everybody else, Trey didn't lean against the wall. Instead, he faced it, staring at the bricks, thinking his thoughts. Mostly, he thought about...bricks.

He liked the geometrical patterns of the mortar-and-brick wall, the neat horizons interrupted by short vertical lines. He imagined a bricklayer assembling the wall on a hot summer day. Maybe the bricklayer's name was Rocco or Gus or Ryan, and his arms were probably hairy. He laid one brick on top of the other, and the other, and the other.

The wall was thick, massive. *It wouldn't be a wall you'd want to run into,* Trey decided. *Though some superheroes could walk through it.* Something about mobilizing the atoms, or re-arranging the particles or molecules or whatever they were called, dissolving into the wall, passing through, and reassembling on a molecular level on the other side. A neat trick, for sure.

What's on the other side of this wall? Trey thought about it, his face close to the bricks. He remembered: the gym! It was right behind this very wall, which was disappointing. If a guy goes to all the trouble of walking through a wall, he'd at least want to get somewhere good. Like Sea World or something. If he walked through a wall, he'd want to see Shamu, the killer whale, not Mr. Z, the smelly gym teacher.

And in this way, Trey Cooper passed the time. He eventually became aware of a close presence, a nearby mass of periwinkle, and the unhappy sound of teeth gnashing on a wad of chewing gum. It was the Queen of Mean. "Trey," she said, "you don't have to stare at the wall. You can turn around and look at everybody else."

She touched his shoulder. Trey shivered, pulled away.

"I like it this way," he murmured.

Trey didn't feel like talking, and nobody could really make him. Besides, he was too busy looking at the bricks. Trey guessed that Mrs. Jenkins probably never *really* looked at bricks. Like most people, she probably thought they were just bricks and that's that.

Most people, Trey realized, just didn't get it.

Trey thought of the colors in his Crayola box. He loved their names and knew them by heart. Staring at the wall, he matched all the colors he saw with his crayons at home. Trey had to start with Red and Orange, just to get those out of the way. Then there were the cheating colors, the ones with hyphens, like Red-Orange and Yellow-

Orange. Trey didn't really like those. After that, it got much better. There were Burnt Orange and Burnt Sienna, Copper and Cranberry, Mahogany and Vivid Tangerine and Cerise. Trey visualized his crayon box at home sitting on his desk in his bedroom. There were Outrageous Orange and Sunset Orange and Salmon and Apricot and a color called Bittersweet.

There used to be a color called Flesh, but in 1962 — the same year that Wilt Chamberlain scored one hundred points — the name got changed to Peach. Trey had read about that once. It made perfect sense to him. People were different. They came in all colors and shapes. You couldn't say that one color was Flesh, and Trey thought it was really dumb of the Crayola people to make that mistake.

Naming crayons was a tricky business. One color name that Trey did not like at all was Fuzzy Wuzzy Brown. That sounded way too babyish. It made it seem like crayons were only for little kids, and Trey knew that wasn't true. Everybody liked to color. It was peaceful. Maybe he should write them a letter....

"Trey? Are you listening?"

The Queen of Mean still stood close to him, looking very round and periwinkle. She sighed heavily, her hot breath warming the back of Trey's neck. "Very well, then," she relented. "Please yourself, Trey. I don't suppose there's a rule against it."

CHAPTER SEVEN

Things Change

While Trey and Ryan stood at the wall, the basketball players scattered across the yard. Some found new games; others talked in small groups.

"This stinks," Billy complained to Spider. "We were having a great game until you invited *him*."

Spider was not in the mood for it. Everything had gone wrong. The problem was, Spider wasn't sure who to blame. It wasn't Trey's fault that he was no good at basketball. But what was with that crazy move at the end, when he kicked the ball into the sky? What was up with that?

It was almost as if Trey was *trying* to make Ryan angry.

"Why are you friends with Trey, anyway?" Billy asked, interrupting Spider's thoughts.

"He's my neighbor," Spider answered. "What am I supposed to do? Run away from him?"

Kurt snickered. "Dude, that might not be a bad idea."

Spider didn't comment. Were they friends, really? Or was it something else, a used-to-be piece of the past? Maybe Spider needed to stop worrying about Trey. It's not like Trey was his brother or anything. They were neighbors. That was it.

Trey had to find his own way. None of it was Spider's fault.

Even so, Spider and Trey had always been friends outside of school. Even when they had different teachers in third and fourth grade, the boys would find each other out back in the narrow strip of woods behind their homes. Trey was forever hammering nails into wood, building things, while Spider climbed trees and hung upside down from sturdy limbs.

Last summer, Trey had become Totally Obsessed With Birds. He always had a pair of binoculars pressed against his eyes as he followed the flight of some backyard bird. You could say that bird-watching was Trey's hobby, the way swimming might be a hobby for a goldfish.

Sometimes the boys sat together in the secret backyard fort, their cockeyed construction of plywood, two-by-fours, old rugs, and spare parts. On dusky afternoons, Spider and Trey often glimpsed a troop of wild turkeys as they cautiously crossed the field that bordered the thicket. The birds were nervous, watchful, thin-legged and ruffle-rumped, somehow weird and a little scary. The turkeys always took the same path, picking their way through the underbrush, searching for berries, nuts, seeds, insects. The mother turkey kept an eye on her brood. If a young one wandered off or fell too far behind the rest, she would go after the youngling, cluck-ing as turkeys do, *keow-keow*. They looked out for each other that way.

"Awesome," Spider would whisper to Trey.

Trey would nod, watching the high-stepping creatures in wide-eyed wonder.

Once Trey murmured, "I wonder if they'll make it."

"What do you mean?" Spider asked.

"Those turkeys need space," Trey told Spider. "But it's getting too crowded around here. Too many houses. Pretty soon, there won't be anywhere for the turkeys to go."

Spider often thought about that conversation, as he did now, standing on the playground with Billy and Kurt. There was something about the way Trey looked at those turkeys, the way he identified with them. They were rare and strange and wonderful.

A whistle blew in short bursts, calling Spider out of his daydreams. It was time to head back inside. As he and his classmates trickled through the doorway, Ava Bright caught up with Spider. He figured she was Pretty Much Okay for a new kid. Weird glasses, but nice.

"What happened with your friend on the basketball court?" Ava asked.

Spider shook his head. He was tired of being asked about Trey, like he was some kind of expert. "I wish everyone would stop calling him my friend. He's just..."

There was something in Ava's eyes that made Spider stop in mid-sentence.

"Really?" Ava asked, puzzled. "I always thought you two were friends."

Then her expression changed. The corners of Ava's mouth turned down, her eyes narrowed. "Oh, I get it now," she said. "But I think you've got it backward. Trey is your friend. It's just that I guess maybe you're not his."

"Whatever," Spider remarked, annoyed. He was frustrated with himself, with Trey, with that big ape Ryan Donovan for making everything worse. Why did Ryan have to act like Mr. Basketball all the time? Spider pulled up at the water fountain, letting Ava and the others pass.

Three times that afternoon he had denied his friendship with Trey Cooper. Three times. Spider took a long drink at the fountain.

Something would have to change.

CHAPTER EIGHT

Try Not To Be So Weird

Alone in the backyard fort, Trey held up a pair of binoculars and scanned the treetops.

Trey and Spider had built the fort last summer, and they shared it without quarrel. It was their private getaway. Entrenched two feet into the earth (the boys dug for three solid days, bone-tired and happy as pigs in mud), the fort rose up a few feet aboveground. It stood about ten feet square. They had hauled in scraps of carpet and sleeping bags and assorted household junk in an effort to make it feel like home. They even got roofing shingles from Spider's dad to keep the rain out. On nice days, like today, they could just slide the roof off, because it was really nothing more than the top of the box. Spider jokingly called it "the retractable dome," like in big sports arenas.

The fort was Trey's favorite place for animal watching, since it kept him safely hidden out of sight. Now Trey picked up a tattered book, a field guide to birds of Eastern North America. He leafed through the pages, brought his nose close to study an illustration, then raised the binoculars again, pushing them through a slot in the wall.

"See anything?"

Trey flinched, startled by Spider's voice. Then his face relaxed into a smile. "Yes," he answered.

Trey climbed out of the fort to join Spider on a fallen log they had dragged over one hot July afternoon. Spider called it "the office."

Trey pointed to a picture in the field guide. "*Vermivora pinus*, the blue-winged warbler," he said. "*Shhh*, listen. Hear that song? It's sort of a *buzzy beeee-bzzz, beeee-bzzz*. Hear it?"

Spider listened, shrugged. "That's him, huh?"

Trey nodded with satisfaction. "Or her," he answered. "In this species, the males and females are nearly identical. They winter in Mexico and Panama."

"Sweet," Spider replied, shifting uneasily on the fallen log. "In the winter we're stuck in the cold and snow, while those birds hang out on the beach in Cancun."

"I haven't seen our turkeys today," Trey noted, scanning the field. "I hope they're okay. My mom saw them last week trying to cross Laurel Road. She had to stop her car to let them pass."

Spider stared out at the field. He sighed. "That was kind of a bad scene at school today," he commented in a way that almost sounded casual. "I'm sorry I got you involved."

"I wanted to play," Trey noted.

"Yeah, well, maybe that wasn't such a hot idea."

Trey looked at Spider's knee, blue jeans and grass stains. "Ryan said I wasn't trying, but I was trying," Trey said. "For a while, anyway. But then you guys stopped passing the ball to me. So, well…"

Trey found a small, round stone on the ground. He picked it up, held it between his thumb and the crook of his index finger. It felt smooth and warm: a lucky rock. He deposited it in his pants pocket. He confessed, "I didn't think Ryan would get so mad."

"That's Ryan. He takes sports pretty seriously," Spider said. He continued with new urgency in his voice. "You can't do that stuff at school. Everybody thinks you're…" His voice trailed off, leaving the words unsaid.

Trey picked up another stone. It was jagged and rough. Worthless. He tossed it away. "Everybody thinks…what?" He scanned the ground for more stones. Lucky ones, hopefully.

"Oh, come on, Trey. You know how those guys are," Spider complained. "Sometimes you cause these problems for yourself. It's like you don't care what people think."

Trey shrugged. He didn't know about that.

He cared plenty. "You want me to be like everybody else? Well, I don't know how to do that," he confessed. "I wish I could, you know. But then there are other times, like today on the playground, when I'm not even sure I *want* to be like everybody else. They think I'm some kind of loser. I just gave them what they expected."

"You did that on purpose?"

Trey shrugged.

Spider snorted and shook his head. "You're crazy, you know that?" He laughed out loud.

Trey smiled. He wasn't sure what was so funny, but it was nice to hear Spider laugh. "I guess I don't know how to be like Ryan Donovan."

"That's not what I meant," Spider replied. He wasn't laughing anymore. He held out his hands, almost as if he were pleading. "I know you can't be *exactly* like everybody in school, Trey. I just wish you'd try not to be so weird."

Spider frowned. The conversation wasn't going the way he had hoped. But it was like a big boulder rolling down a hill. There was no stopping it. "It's cool that we hang out at home," Spider continued. He rubbed the palms of his hands against his jeans. "But do you think that maybe, you know, in school, you could...chill out a little bit?"

Trey kept searching for stones in the dirt. He listened to his heart, *ba-thump, ba-thump, ba-thump*. He thought about getting up and going inside for a drink of cranberry juice or whatever. He could feel Spider's eyes looking at him and sensed that Spider was waiting for a reply. "What do you mean?" Trey asked.

"I can't always hang out with you at school," Spider pointed out. "I need more space. On the playground, in the lunchroom, walking back and forth from school together every day. You have to learn how to take care of yourself, Trey."

Trey nodded, thinking it over. He told himself that he wasn't upset. He was just trying to wrap his mind around it, trying to understand what Spider was saying.

"We can still be friends," Spider added. "We'll still hang out and everything —"

"You want to be friends," Trey interrupted, "but just not when anybody else is around."

"No, I didn't say that!" Spider protested.

"That's okay," Trey said. "Around here, we'll be friends. But in school...maybe not so much?"

Spider seemed to deflate a little, the air leaking out of him. He looked out across the empty field.

Trey lifted the binoculars and focused on Spider, who sat only three feet away. All he saw was a peach-colored blur.

"I can't be your only friend in the world, Trey," Spider tried to explain.

Trey nodded, as if it made perfect sense. He set down the binoculars. They were beginning to give him a headache. Then he said, "Why not?"

"Um...what?"

"Why not?" Trey repeated. "I don't need a million-zillion friends."

Spider exhaled. After a long pause, he said, "People are like chairs."

"They are?"

"And friends are like the legs of the chair,"

Spider added. "You can't have a chair with only one leg, can you?"

Trey found another stone in the dirt. It was smooth and white and felt solid in his hand. He liked it immediately.

"Even with two legs," Spider went on, "a chair would be too wobbly."

"Some stools have only three legs," Trey noted, bargaining.

"Right," Spider said. "Three legs. Okay, sure. That's how many friends you need."

Trey looked away. *Three friends. Hmmm.* He was a couple short. A movement in the field caught his eye. A red-tailed hawk came tearing down from the clouds, talons out and murder in its heart, dive-bombing to kill a chipmunk or rabbit. Wow. Trey raised his binoculars and watched.

The conversation was over.

Spider stood up, stretched. "Hey, I'm going to shoot baskets in my driveway." He paused. "Do you want to come?"

"I suck at basketball," Trey reminded him.

Spider shrugged and smiled. "It's okay, it's just us. We can play H-O-R-S-E. If one guy hits a shot, the other guy has to make the same shot. If you miss, you get a letter. First one to spell H-O-R-S-E loses."

Trey remembered that game. He liked trying to make crazy shots. You could miss and nobody got mad. "Let's play F-A-R-T-S instead," Trey suggested.

"Farts?"

"Same number of letters," Trey explained, "funnier word."

Spider reached out a hand and pulled Trey up from the ground. Six white stones rattled in Trey's pocket—each one of them lucky.

"Thanks for your help!" Trey said, remembering the poster in Mrs. Wine's classroom.

And it worked. Spider smiled.

Now Trey just needed to find two more friends, and life would be a lot less wobbly.

CHAPTER NINE

Trouble Coming

Quarter to nine the next morning, Spider set off for school. He passed by Trey's and, out of habit, almost turned up the front walk to knock on the door. But he resisted, forcing himself not to look at the house. Spider wondered if Trey was watching from a window, peering at the back of Spider's head. He tried not to think about it.

At school, things went pretty well. For a while, anyway. Spider noticed that Trey stayed away from him all through morning classes and during snack break. Even so, Spider's eyes kept returning to Trey, watching with sideways glances, waiting for something to happen. He didn't know what he expected. To Spider, the whole day felt like he was standing behind a horse. Everything seemed okay enough, but Spider kept wondering when he might step in something or get kicked in the head.

He didn't have to wonder for long.

When Spider sat down in the lunchroom, he could see trouble coming. After all, he had lived next door to Trey Cooper all his life; Spider knew trouble when he saw it. He had already grabbed a seat with a group of boys from class. But there was an empty chair next to him at the table. And now up came Trey Cooper in that dreamy flat-footed way of his, missing all the signs, eyes fixed on the empty chair.

Don't, Spider thought. *Find somewhere else, Trey. Not today, not now. Give me a break.*

The chair scraped across the floor. Trey sat down, not saying anything. He just gave Spider an awkward thumbs-up.

"Hey," Spider mumbled, barely above a whisper. Not a greeting—a warning.

"Hello, Spider," Trey replied, his voice too loud.

Spider shifted in his chair, inching away. He eyed the other guys at the table, chomping on sandwiches like they hadn't eaten in days. A couple of them, Ryan Donovan and Billy Timmons, had stopped mid-chew, mouths hanging open. They watched Trey in disapproval.

Trey laid out the contents of his lunch: a cup of diced peaches, a ham sandwich, a drink, and a Tupperware container filled with some kind of gross-looking yogurt.

"What's that you're eating, Cooper?" Ryan snapped. "It looks like cat vomit."

Billy snorted. The other boys joined in, too. Cat vomit, good one, yuk-yuk. Spider slouched in his chair. Ryan wasn't going to let things go. He was like a dog with a bone—and Trey was the bone. Spider wanted to roll up a newspaper and whack Ryan on the nose.

Instead, he did nothing.

Trey glanced down at his yogurt, sprinkled

with wheat germ, flaxseed, and whatever other healthful ingredients his mother had included. Trey's mother was always trying to get him to eat healthy foods, and now look what it got him. A big fat bull's-eye on his back. Ryan was right. It *did* look like cat vomit.

"You gonna lick that up?" Ryan asked.

"Well, it does look kind of bad," Trey agreed. "Sort of like your face, Donovan."

Trey smiled, beaming, eyes darting around the table, waiting for the laughter.

None came.

"What did you say?" Ryan snarled. His big hands twitched on the table.

Trey didn't answer. He looked away.

"Huh? I asked you a question, Cooper."

Spider spoke up. "Um, maybe it's time to —"

"Why don't you take a hike, Trey?" Ryan said, ignoring Spider. His voice was filled with threat. "Nobody wants you here. Take your cat vomit and go away."

Ryan looked around the table, grinning, nodding his thick bowling-ball skull. He looked to Spider, at that moment, like a bulldog. A big, dumb dog on a chain that you shouldn't get too close to.

"You just cause trouble," Kurt said quietly to Trey, by way of an explanation. "It would be better for everybody if you just sat somewhere else."

"Better for everybody?" Trey echoed. He turned from Kurt to Spider. "I never meant —"

"Like at recess yesterday," Justin Seo chimed in, his mouth clogged with food. "No basketball for a week. All because of you."

"Like at...everywhere," Ryan said.

Trey stood abruptly. His movement was awkward and sudden, his eyes downcast, not meeting anyone's gaze. There was stillness at the table, a frozen waiting, the boys wondering what Trey would do next. Ryan stiffened, ready for battle, his fingers curled into fists.

Spider checked the location of the lunch aides. Was Mrs. Jenkins watching? What should he do?

Come to Trey's defense, stay out of it, what? He felt paralyzed, helpless.

But nothing happened. Trey crumpled up his paper napkin, lunch bag, and the rest of his meal. He walked to the garbage cans at the front of the room. Without breaking pace, Trey tossed the garbage away—Tupperware, utensils, and all—and kept right on walking. Flat-footed, arms dangling at his sides, head inclined forward as usual, giving off that uneasy sensation of a boy tumbling forward, forever about to fall. Trey walked past Mrs. Jenkins, out the door, and was gone.

Mrs. Jenkins's eyes widened, staring from Trey back to the table, confused and suspicious. She called after Trey with a high-pitched hiss, snapping her fingers. "Excuse me, Mr. Cooper? Mr. Cooper? Do you have a pass, young man?"

Maybe Trey didn't hear, for he often didn't. But it was more likely that Trey heard the noon aide's calls and simply didn't care.

CHAPTER TEN

Flying

The moment he stepped into the hallway, a sense of relief washed over Trey. He had escaped.

The hallway was nice, empty and echoing. He followed his feet along the tiled path, turned left, then right, pushed open a door, and entered the library. Ms. Lobel sat behind the counter, speaking with a couple of second graders. She saw Trey and gave a nod, then returned her attention to the pint-size students.

The computers against the wall were already occupied; about half a dozen other kids sat at nearby tables, leafing through books and talking quietly. A few wandered among the shelves, fingers on the spines of hardcovers, searching for something to read. Trey found a stuffed chair in the back corner, hidden by a high bookshelf. He plopped down, hands on his lap, closed his eyes, and almost instantly fell asleep.

Trey dreamed. And in his dream he felt that tug again, so he rose and stepped outside under the pale stars of the night sky. The air was cool and smelled of pine and moved like a panther from rock to rock. Trey felt a tingling in his fingertips, as if the hands at his sides were sparrows aflutter. The dew licked his toes as he stepped onto the lawn. He closed his eyes and waited.

First the world fell away, slipped off him like a shed skin. He filled his senses with sounds and smells. Then it came, that feathery feeling in his stomach, his body filling with the lightness of helium, his skin stretched thin like a balloon, and he lifted into the air, hovering inches above the earth. His eyes were closed. The smell of decayed leaves and the corpses of flowers filled his nostrils. And he lifted higher, floating above the ground, his house below him now, trees beneath his feet. He was in the sky, flying, a kite riding the currents....

"Trey?"

There was a hand on his shoulder.

"Trey?"

How? Who?

Ms. Lobel, the librarian, stood before him. "You've been sleeping."

Trey blinked himself awake. "How long?"

"You've had quite a nap," Ms. Lobel informed him. "It's almost time to go home."

"What?!" Trey rose to his feet, head still in the clouds. "I was dreaming."

"*Shhh*, it's okay," Ms. Lobel reassured him. She touched his arm. "We decided to let you sleep."

"We?" Trey asked.

"I spoke with Mrs. Wine and the school counselor, Mr. Rice. We all decided it would be best to let you sleep. I understand that you've had a rough couple of days." Ms. Lobel smiled. "Are you thirsty? Would you like a cup of water?"

Trey looked around. The library was empty.

The wall clock read 3:10. There were only fifteen minutes left in the school day. A panic came over him. "I missed geography and—"

"It's fine, Trey," Ms. Lobel said. Her voice was soft, gentle. She handed Trey a slip of paper. "I've written a pass for you. You can always come here, Trey, if you ever need a quiet place."

Trey glanced at the shelves that lined the walls, the new books, the smooth polished tabletops that smelled of Lemon Pledge, the chairs tucked in and neatly arranged. "I can?" he asked.

Ms. Lobel parted her lips, full as ripe strawberries, and smiled. "Not *all* the time," she said, grinning. "But we all need a quiet place every now and then—especially during lunchtime and recess, when things can get a little wild. You are always welcome here, Trey."

She pressed a sealed note into Trey's hand. "Please give this to Mrs. Wine," Ms. Lobel said.

Trey shot her a doubtful look.

"It's all right, Trey. We're all on your side," she

reassured him. "Now get going or you'll miss the final bell."

Trey nodded, a little stunned. On the way out the door, he paused and turned. "Ms. Lobel," he said, "you rock."

The red-haired librarian smiled.

CHAPTER 11

Green Hair

The last couple of days, things had changed. Spider felt different. He felt...well, he couldn't find a word for exactly how he felt. It was more like a picture. And, okay, it was sort of a gross way of looking at it, but Spider just couldn't get the image out of his head. It was like there had been a sumo wrestler standing on his chest and now, suddenly, the fat man was gone. For the first time in days, Spider felt like he could breathe. Like this: *phew*.

Maybe that was the word. *Phew*. Spider wasn't even sure if that *was* a real word. It seemed more like a sound. What did Mrs. Wine call that?

Onomatopoeia. Like *pssst,* and *whirr,* and *blat!* No Trey, no sumo wrestler standing on Spider's chest. *Phew.*

Trey seemed to be doing better lately. The week had started rough, but things had been quiet the past two days. Spider started to think about other things. It was Friday, and that was *always* a good thing. Even better, Spider planned to go home on the bus with Kurt and a couple of other guys. They were going to play ball, order pizza, and rent a movie. Spider had never been to Kurt's house. It was All Good.

He arrived at school a few minutes before the bell. Mrs. Wine sat at her desk, chatting with Cissy and Jess Ames. The morning sun poured through the windows, filling the room with light. Spider joined Kurt and Justin, who lounged on beanbag chairs in the reading corner.

"S'up," Justin said, lifting his chin a half inch in greeting.

"Hey, Spider. Are you still coming over after school today?" Kurt asked.

"Yep," Spider replied. Real cool, like it didn't mean anything.

"Sweet," Kurt replied. "If Ryan comes, we can practice a few plays for the Hoops for Heart tournament. It's coming up next week, you know."

Ryan Donovan, Spider thought. He wasn't so sure about that kid.

Kurt must have seen the doubt flicker across Spider's face. "Ryan is a good guy," Kurt assured him. "He just gets a little worked up sometimes. He's a great basketball player."

"I know," Spider replied, even though he didn't.

Suddenly a buzz swept through the room. "Wow, look at Trey!" Kurt exclaimed.

Spider turned and saw Trey, surrounded by a group of classmates. His hair was bright green.

"Trey! What did you do?" Olive asked.

"I dyed it," Trey answered. He seemed pleased with himself.

"It looks freaky," Samantha Kim said.

Trey shrugged.

"Why green?" Leah Papadopoulos asked.

79

"It was supposed to be Caribbean Green—that's what the label said—but I think it came out more like Electric Lime," Trey explained. His fingers touched the side of his head. "I like it, though."

After a minute or two, most kids just sort of drifted back to what they had been doing. If everyone on the planet was due for fifteen minutes of fame, as the artist Andy Warhol once predicted, then Trey was still owed twelve minutes and thirty-two seconds.

"I think you look more like a Granny Smith apple," Spider observed, walking toward Trey with a wry grin on his face.

"Do you like it?" Trey asked.

"Yeah, sure, I guess," Spider answered, not altogether truthfully. "I mean, it's different, but—"

Ava Bright interrupted. "Well, I think it looks fabulous, Trey! How did you do it?"

"With a spray can," Trey answered. "Something called Color Bombz."

"Oh, I love that stuff!" Ava squealed. She

clapped her hands and recited in a deep voice, "Color Bombz — for fun hair with flair!"

Trey laughed. "Yeah, that's what it says on the can."

"They *say* it's temporary," Ava warned him, "but you'll have to wash it a few times before you get rid of all the green."

"I don't mind."

"I tried pink once," Ava confided. "My friends and I did it at a sleepover party where I used to live. My head looked like cotton candy!"

"Really?"

"Yes, it was shocking pink! My mother freaked!" Ava said, glancing from Trey to Spider, grinning at the memory.

Spider could see that Trey seemed at ease around Ava. More like himself. That's when Spider noticed Ava's jewelry. She was wearing... feather earrings. No wonder Trey liked her.

When Ava walked away, Spider elbowed Trey. "Did you check out her earrings?"

Trey blushed. Yes, he saw.

CHAPTER 12

Ms. Lobel

Trey carried his lunch to the library later that same day.

"I'm here," he announced, holding up a salami sandwich. He handed Ms. Lobel a pink sheet of paper. "Mrs. Wine said it was okay. Is it…" he asked, hesitating, "…still okay?"

The young, long-haired librarian glanced at the permission slip and tucked it into her pocket. "Trey, you have perfect timing," she said. "This is my free period. I was just on my way to the teachers' lounge."

"Oh," Trey replied. His eyes fell to the floor.

"But I'd much rather stay here and eat with

you," she quickly added. "To tell you the truth, I get nervous in the teachers' lounge."

"You do?"

"Oh yes," Ms. Lobel confided. "It can get so stuffy in there. I never feel quite at home." Her face brightened. "Come, we can eat at my desk."

Trey paused, waiting. Finally he asked, "Ms. Lobel, do you notice anything *new* about me?"

She looked him up and down, finger tapping on her chin. "Your shoes?" she guessed.

Trey frowned.

"Oh, I'm just having fun with you, Trey," the librarian said. "Even a bookworm like me can see that you've dyed your hair!"

Lunch was nice in the library, away from the noise of the lunchroom. Ms. Lobel was a good talker. Mostly Trey listened, nodding as she chatted. Ms. Lobel loved dogs and swimming in lakes and long books on rainy days. Her real name was Hildreth, but her friends called her Hil or Hildy.

When it was his turn to talk, Trey listed all the

birds he had recently spotted in his backyard. "Let's see, what have I said so far? There was the house finch, the pine grosbeak, the golden-crowned sparrow, all sorts of warblers, a gray catbird, a northern mockingbird—"

"Would you like my Oreos, Trey?" Ms. Lobel finally interrupted, her lips pulled into a smile. "I don't think I can finish my dessert."

Thus distracted, Trey looked up and answered that he would very much like her Oreos. The last crumb eaten, Trey stated matter-of-factly: "Spider says that people are like chairs, but I think they are more like stools. What do you think, Ms. Lobel?"

The librarian appeared confused. "What do I...what? Like stools?"

Trey explained Spider's theory of friendship. How everybody needed at least three friends or else they got too wobbly and fell down.

"Your friend Spider certainly has some interesting ideas," Ms. Lobel mused.

"He's only my part-time friend," Trey pointed out. "At home we are friends. But in school…not so much."

Ms. Lobel frowned. "Too cool for school, is that it?"

"Beats me," Trey replied. "Ms. Lobel, can I ask you something?"

"You just did, and you certainly may."

Trey blinked, trying to process what she'd just said. "How do you make friends, exactly?"

"Exactly? Oh my," Ms. Lobel clucked. "That's a tough question, Trey."

"That's why I asked."

Ms. Lobel smiled. Her eyes were soft and dark, like round stones in a stream. She gestured to the bookshelves. "Look at all these books. Each one is unique. And whenever a student walks through that door, I'm absolutely positive that somewhere in here is a book that's right for that child." She paused. "Do you know what I mean?"

"Nope," Trey admitted.

Ms. Lobel laughed. She did that a lot. "I'm sure

there are friends out there who are just right for you."

"Like books," Trey said.

"Right," Ms. Lobel agreed. "So now you have to ask yourself, what kind of people do you like?"

Trey had never thought about it that way before. Finding a friend was like picking a book. He considered Ms. Lobel's question. He liked birds, but Trey decided that birds could not count as friends. "I guess I like people who are nice, and, oh yeah, who maybe have…feathers," he added.

"Feathers?"

"Like on their clothes or something," Trey said.

"I see," Ms. Lobel murmered, though by the way she scratched her head it didn't seem like she saw at all. "I think looking for nice people would be a good place to start. In my experience, nice people often make the best friends."

A class filed into the library. "You'll have to excuse me now, Trey. It's time for you to head back to Mrs. Wine's room."

Without another word, Trey stood, turned, and walked away. But at the door he thought of one last thing he needed to say about his hair. "It was supposed to be Caribbean Green, but I think maybe it looks more like Electric Lime. But that's okay. Ava Bright's hair came out like cotton candy. You just never know how these things will turn out. Thanks again for lunch!"

CHAPTER 13

Ava Bright

During a quiet moment in the afternoon, Spider turned to steal a better look at Trey.

Trey returned Spider's gaze, a lopsided grin on his face.

"Why did you do it?" Spider whispered.

Trey puffed out his cheeks, then pushed them with his hands. "I'm building a stool," he said, nodding knowingly. "Right now, I'm trying to decide if librarians count."

"A stool?" Spider echoed.

"You know, three friends," Trey reminded him, holding up three fingers. "So I won't be so wobbly anymore."

"Oh, right. So...you dyed your hair green?"

Trey nodded enthusiastically. "I thought it might give me a little pizzazz — and do you know what? It worked!"

Spider wasn't so sure. "Really?"

Green-haired Trey slid his eyes sideways. "Ava," he intoned.

Before Spider could reply, Mrs. Wine said without looking up from her desk, "I'm glad you are already finished with your geography work, Trey. But please keep your voice down. Others may not be so fortunate."

Spider had to hand it to Mrs. Wine. She didn't miss much. It must be those eyes in the back of her head. Spider would have to write a story about that someday. It might involve an alien spaceship.

During Writer's Workshop, Spider eagerly pulled out his journal. He had another idea that he'd been thinking about. He sketched a picture of Trey Cooper, alone on a football field, lined up against six massive football players. He scribbled the caption: "Play nice, boys." Then Spider filled almost two pages with writing before Mrs. Wine called him to the back table. He had written about the argument between Trey and Ryan.

Spider handed his journal to Mrs. Wine. He explained sheepishly, "You did say we could write about *anything*. I know we're not supposed to do pictures, but..."

Spider fell silent when Mrs. Wine took the journal, held up a finger for quiet, and began reading. Finally, she raised her face and smiled. "I like it. Some of these drawings are really funny, Spider. I'm glad you added them to your journal, so long as you don't neglect your writing." She turned another page and read silently. "You have very good observation skills, Spider. That's the mark of a good writer. You *see* things."

They talked about Spider's interest in graphic novels. Mrs. Wine admitted that she didn't know much about them, but she was willing to learn. Spider thought of the expression, *You can't teach an old dog new tricks*. But he was smart enough not to mention it. He agreed to loan the books to Mrs. Wine anyway. Because, hey, you never know!

At the end of their session, Mrs. Wine gathered her papers. In a soft voice that could not be overheard, she asked, "Are you all set for Hoops for Heart?"

"Yes," he answered. "I'm teaming up with Kurt and Ryan."

"Oh, I see," she said. "I was asking because I'm trying to help a couple of students find a team."

Spider tensed. He knew who she was worried about.

Mrs. Wine continued, "I was hoping that you'd be willing to play with Trey."

"I can't," Spider answered. He put a frown on his face as if he meant it. There was no way he wanted to play in a basketball tournament with Trey Cooper. Nope, not going to happen. It was too much.

"I understand," she said. "You already made a commitment."

"That's right," Spider replied. There was no

choice, really. It didn't make him a bad guy or anything.

Mrs. Wine wished Spider good luck.

And that was that. He had his own life to live. Spider couldn't spend every minute worrying about Trey Cooper.

But for some reason, he did. The problem gnawed at him all day. Until he realized that maybe — just maybe — he could help after all.

At the end of the school day, Spider found his moment. He spied Ava Bright alone by the cubbies. Along came Spider. "Hey, Ava," he said, casually grabbing his backpack. "What are you doing, like, this Saturday?"

"Tomorrow?" Ava said. "I don't know. Why?"

Spider scratched the back of his neck. He glanced in the direction of Trey. "I was wondering," he said. "Do you, um, like birds...?"

And so at eleven A.M. on Saturday morning, Ava Bright rang the doorbell at Spider's house. She wore jeans, a tie-dyed shirt, a corduroy shirt over that, and her usual thick eyeglasses. Her hair was piled high in what looked to Spider like a big knot. He would never understand girls and their hair. Why didn't they just wear baseball caps?

He stepped out on the front stoop, shutting the door behind him. "Thanks for coming."

Ava looked around uncertainly. "Can I leave my skateboard here?"

"Yeah, sure, that's fine." Spider felt a sense of panic settle in his stomach, as if he had eaten a burned marshmallow. What had he gotten himself into? Why couldn't he leave things alone? This was *his* idea, his Grand Master Plan, but now Spider feared it was a terrible mistake. After all, it depended on Trey. *Anything* could happen when Trey was involved — and it usually did.

"Is he back there?" Ava asked. She tilted her head toward the backyard.

"Yeah, we have to go around the other side. That's his house, next door. Trey should be there now."

They found green-haired Trey sprawled on his

back patio. He was on his knees, hunched over scraps of wood and various tools — measuring tape, saw, hammer, drill, chisel, screwdrivers.

Ava's eyes widened as she took in the entire backyard, the stand of breathtaking oaks, maples, and pines, the field of wild grass beyond. She arched her back and gazed up at the great old trees. "This is really, really nice," she murmured.

Trey scrambled to his feet. "Oh, hi. I didn't hear you guys."

"What are you building?" Ava asked.

"A gift," Trey answered. "It's a nest box."

"A nest box?"

"Most people call them birdhouses," Trey said, "but most people are wrong."

Spider grinned. He had heard Trey recite facts about birds and nest boxes many times. It was amazing and, at the same time, So Totally Out There. Trey could sit for hours in perfect silence, but when he got going on one of his favorite topics — like birds or rocks or ice cream — he would talk nonstop. And it didn't matter if you paid attention or not. It was as if Trey had so many facts crammed into his head, he couldn't keep them locked inside. Spider imagined a volcano spewing hot lava: Mount Trey.

"Can I help?" Ava asked. "I mean, I don't know anything about nest boxes, but I'm pretty good with a hammer."

Trey nodded, sure she could help. He looked at Spider with a question in his eyes.

"Sounds good to me," Spider said.

Trey showed them what to do. And while he did, he explained things to Ava, who was either astonishingly polite or very interested — or both. "About one hundred different species of birds nest in natural cavities," Trey said. "You know, like holes in trees, the eaves of houses, things like that."

Ava nodded, listening as she made measurements on a length of pine board.

"But lots of trees are cut down every year," Trey said. "That's bad for birds. Their natural habitat is shrinking. Plus, other animals — like squirrels, which I *do not* like"—he said with surprising hostility—"all compete for the nesting places. Lots of songbirds like nest boxes. Bluebirds, titmice, chickadees, wrens—"

"It's nice that you build them," Ava said. "I'm sure the birds appreciate it."

"Well, we have to take care of them, don't we?" Trey said matter-of-factly. "I mean, they can't build these by themselves. And it's so easy for us."

Even though Spider had heard Trey say things like that many times before, this time the words struck him a different way. *We have to take care of them, don't we?* It was a simple thing to say. A clear, true thought. *We have to take care of them,* Spider repeated to himself. *It's so easy for us.*

The clouds parted and a warm yellow sun shone down. Ava, Trey, and Spider worked together for the next couple of hours, laughing and talking. Ava asked a lot of questions—she had a curious, interested sort of mind—and Trey had all the answers. He explained how the nest box roof needed at least three inches of overhang to protect the birds from hard rain. He showed Ava how to spread a coat of petroleum jelly along the inside of the roof to keep away wasps and bees. And with a chisel, Trey patiently grooved the interior walls of the house. "It helps the baby birds climb to the opening," he explained.

Ava was impressed. She looked around, suddenly puzzled. "But I only count two nest boxes in your yard," she said. "I thought you built lots of them?"

"I give them away," Trey explained. "Birds are territorial. They don't like it if you put the boxes too close together. They don't like crowds, and I totally agree with them," he said. Trey finished screwing the last galvanized screw into the nest box. "There," he said proudly, holding up the final creation.

"You're very talented, Trey," Ava said with admiration. "And smart. Isn't he, Spider?"

"He's one of a kind," Spider replied, grinning.

"I'm giving this one to Ms. Lobel," Trey announced.

"The school librarian?"

"Yeah, she's my friend." It was true.

The three of them ate a late lunch on the picnic table and later explored the nearby field, searching for snakes and rabbit warrens. To Spider's surprise, Ava knew a lot about nature from reading all those Survival Handbooks. She could probably survive the winter on roots and berries.

Ava suggested painting the nest box, but Trey didn't think that was a good idea. "It has to be nontoxic paint," he told her.

"Maybe next time," Ava said. "I can get some nontoxic paint from home. I have tons of art supplies. Would that be okay?"

Trey said that it would be.

Spider commented that it was Mighty Big of Trey to let Ava donate her art supplies. Ava laughed, but Trey didn't seem to get it.

"We could decorate some of them, you know, just for fun," Ava suggested. "Maybe glue on little pieces of broken mirror, stones, glitter. We could turn the nest boxes into art."

Trey wasn't sure about that. "Birds aren't interested in art," he noted.

Ava shrugged, unconvinced. "Think about it."

All the while, Spider sat back, relaxed and pleased. He happily faded into the background while Ava and Trey talked. Ava had a special gift; she was easy to be around. It was hard to explain. She just had a nice way about her. The day had gone better than he expected. Which wasn't so hard to believe, since he had expected a train wreck.

Out of nowhere, Trey asked Ava, "Do you play basketball?"

Uh-oh, thought Spider. *Houston, we have a problem!*

"Play it? I'm a superstar," Ava bragged. "My uncle Earl from Swampy Flats, Louisiana, used to play in the NBA!"

"Really?" Spider chimed in, impressed.

Ava laughed. "No, I made that up. Actually, he sells life insurance. His name is Fred Sugarman. And he's from New Jersey. When it comes to sports, my whole family is a bunch of klutzes."

"Me, too!" Trey exclaimed. "We should start a team together!"

Why didn't I think of that? Spider thought sarcastically. *Get the worst players in the school and make a team. Genius.*

But right then and there, Trey and Ava decided to team up for Hoops for Heart. "We'll need one more player," Ava mused. "What do you think, Spider? Want to join us?"

"I, um, can't. Sorry, I wish I could," Spider said, hoping that his nose wouldn't suddenly grow like Pinnochio's. "I'm already on a team."

"Well, your loss," Ava said, hands on her hips, chin jutting out. "Beware of the Mighty Klutzes. We're going to score more runs than anybody."

"Points," Spider corrected her. "In basketball, you score points. Runs are in baseball."

Ava dismissed him with a wave of her hand. "Don't cloud the issue with facts!" she replied cheerily.

If Spider could be sure of one thing, it was that this was definitely going to be worth seeing.

CHAPTER 14

The Gift

On Monday, Trey visited the library.

"Are you here for lunch, Trey?" Ms. Lobel asked.

"No, thanks. It's a sunny day, and I thought I'd go outside."

"That sounds like an excellent idea. You know where I am if you need me." Ms. Lobel looked from Trey to the large shopping bag he carried. "Okay, I give up. What have you got in there?"

Trey hesitated, suddenly unsure of himself. He reached his hand into the bag and produced the nest box. "I made this for you."

"A birdhouse!" Ms. Lobel exclaimed.

Trey didn't have the heart to tell her that it was

a nest box and that only ignorant people called them birdhouses. He didn't want to spoil the moment. But boy, it wasn't easy.

The look on Ms. Lobel's face helped. Her eyes gleamed, her cheeks flushed, her strawberry mouth smiled wide.

"Oh, Trey, you surprise me."

Trey shrugged. "Sometimes I surprise myself."

"I can't wait to put it up in my yard," Ms. Lobel said. "I've never had a birdhouse before."

She said it again. *Birdhouse.* Trey tried to think of other things, like how sedimentary rocks are formed. Then he listed all the colors in the first row of his crayon box. But finally he couldn't take it any longer.

"They are called nest boxes," he said, maybe a little too loud.

"Oh, dear," Ms. Lobel said, looking startled. "And here I am calling your nice gift a birdhouse — I'm awfully sorry, Trey."

She wasn't smiling anymore.

Trey didn't know what to do next. He had

given Ms. Lobel the gift, but then he'd kind of yelled at her and ruined things. He glanced around the room helplessly.

Then it hit him. "You know," Trey said, "I think a nest box is like this library. It's a safe, clean, quiet place. Maybe that's why I like it here so much. This place is my nest box."

Ms. Lobel placed a hand on her chest. "That's a lovely thought, Trey."

The smile was back where it belonged, dancing across Ms. Lobel's face.

"I wanted to thank you," Trey mumbled to the carpet.

"You are very welcome, Trey. I'm truly touched by your kindness."

"I know," Trey replied. He glanced at the wall clock. "I have to go. Ava is saving me a seat in the lunchroom. If I eat super quick, we can get outside to practice our basketball skills," he explained.

Trey told Ms. Lobel about Ava, and Hoops for Heart, and their team, the Mighty Klutzes. "We still need one more person. I tried all the kids in room 511. But I don't think anybody wants to team up with a couple of klutzes."

"I'll play on your team," Ms. Lobel offered.

"What?"

"I love basketball," she said. "I was hoping that someone would ask me to play, but nobody ever did. I played college ball, you know."

"Does that mean you used to be good?" Trey asked.

Ms. Lobel made a face. "I'm actually *still* pretty good. I'm only twenty-five years old, Trey. It's not like I'm an old lady."

"Oh." Trey scratched his left elbow.

"I don't know if I qualify for your team," Ms. Lobel said. A worried look flickered in her eyes. "Strictly speaking, I'm not a klutz."

"Well," Trey considered. "I *guess* it's okay. I mean, you don't *have* to be awful, Ms. Lobel. It's not like there's a rule or anything. Me and Ava don't care. We won't hold it against you if you don't stink."

"I'm so happy to hear you say that."

"I should probably ask Ava first," Trey said after a pause. "You know, to see if it's all right with her."

Ms. Lobel's eyes twinkled. "It sounds like you've made a friend."

Trey shrugged. What could he say? It was true. Now he had two friends: Ava Bright and Ms. Hildreth Lobel, the college basketball star.

He also had one part-time friend named Spider Stevens.

Trey walked out the door, wondering if two and a half friends might be enough.

CHAPTER 15

Heart

The rest of the week went fast, like an arrow flying to its target. Everything seemed to be pointing to Saturday and the Hoops for Heart lollapalooza. That was Trey's new favorite word of the week: *lollapalooza*. It meant that something was wonderful and amazing. But Trey didn't care what the word defined. He just liked saying it. Over and over again. Olive Desmond, the girl who always complained about Trey's humming, was nearly driven insane by Trey's whispered mumblings: *"...lollapalooza, lolla-palooza, lol-LA-pa-LOO-za!"*

Mrs. Wine had been busy. Trey noticed a new sign up in the class bathroom. The paper was taped to the lower left corner of the mirror and read: *"GOOD HAND WASHING TAKES 20 SECONDS!"* It was in all capital letters, in red marker, and underlined three times because it was such an important message. The note got Trey thinking. It gave him a mission. Each day, he worked to set a new record in a frantic, splashy scramble of soap and water. And by Friday, after much practice, Trey managed the feat in just three seconds. Clean hands! Mrs. Mowatt finally had to ask Trey to please not spend so much class time in the bathroom when there was work to do.

Nothing else much seemed to happen that week, except for one very good thing named Ava Bright.

Trey practiced basketball with Ava during recess. It was magical, the way the orange basketball gave them a chance to be together. They weren't boyfriend and girlfriend or anything creepy like that. But if a ball was there, tucked in the crook of an elbow, it was okay for Trey and Ava to hang around. Just friends. Once in a while Trey would toss the ball up in the direction of the hoop, not caring if it went in or not. Usually it clanged against the metal backboard with a thud.

Ava was determined to master a new move. For reasons that were not clear to Trey, Ava wanted to spin around while dribbling. She would bounce the ball, spin around lightning fast, and try to keep dribbling. Ava got pretty dizzy that way. Once, she even fell to the ground. It didn't matter; she just laughed and laughed, like it was the funniest thing ever. Ava was like that. Her laughter was like a case of the flu or a really bad cold. Contagious, but without the gross coughing. Trey had to laugh, too.

Trey felt like he had stumbled upon a secret. For the first time, he understood sports. Basketball was just an excuse to be together, running and jumping and doing whatever. It didn't really matter how many points you scored, so long as you made a friend out of the deal. Trey tried to explain his theory to Spider, who shrugged and said, "I guess."

But Ava understood. And by the end of the week, Trey and Ava didn't even need a ball anymore to make their friendship seem okay. It was more comfortable over by the bench swing, anyway, beneath the swaying trees. They told stories, Ava gave Trey survival tips — if a crocodile has you in its jaws, punch it very hard in the end of its snout — and together they looked for stones.

Back in room 511 one afternoon, Mrs. Wine explained to the class that the heart was a muscle. "That's why we need to exercise our hearts. It's how we stay healthy. It is especially good to do things that get us huffing and puffing!"

"Like the Big Bad Wolf," Ryan suggested.

"Yes, I'm sure all that huffing and puffing was very aerobic," Mrs. Wine answered. "The Big Bad Wolf probably had a very healthy heart."

Everybody got a good laugh at that.

Inspired by the laughter, Mrs. Wine told a joke:

"A woman walks into a doctor's office. She looks like a mess," Mrs. Wine said, acting out the story. "There's a carrot jammed up one nostril. There's a cucumber stuck inside the other nostril. And there's a banana in her left ear! 'Doctor, doctor!' she cries. 'What's the matter with me?'

"The doctor answers, 'Obviously, you're not eating properly.'"

Trey laughed until he got the hiccups. (Which really drove Olive Desmond up the wall.)

Here are the other things Trey learned in school that week:

A human heart is about as big as that person's fist, while a blue whale's heart is as big as a car! Trey was not sure what kind of car; he'd have to check on that.

A heart beats about once a second, pumping a river of blood throughout the body. When Trey listened closely, his heart sounded like this: *pum-PUM, pum-PUM, pum-PUM.* They say that a bird's heart goes so fast you can't even count the beats. It sounds like a steady drumroll, *drrrrrrr.*

In an average lifetime, a heart beats something like two billion times. That's not an exact number; it's an estimate, which is another word for "Big Guess." And it looks like this when you write it out: 2,000,000,000!

A heart is not heart-shaped, like people draw on valentine cards. People are wrong about that (again!). A heart looks more like an upside-down pear that's red and bloody and, well, basically disgusting. Trey didn't like to think about it. He decided that in this case it was okay if people made pictures of hearts that were all wrong. A real heart wouldn't look so great on a valentine card. Instead of making someone love you, it would probably make them want to puke. Which totally wasn't the idea.

Back in the times of long ago, people used to think that the heart was the center of everything, the source of all feelings and hopes and dreams. Now, Mrs. Wine explained, scientists believe all that stuff happens in the brain. To them, a heart is just a bag of muscles — valves, veins, and arteries. It made Trey sad, because those scientists turned the heart into nothing but a pump, like a machine you could rent at a hardware store for $29.95, plus tax.

It didn't make sense to Trey.

After all, Saturday was the day of the Hoops for Heart celebration. He was going to play with Ava and Ms. Lobel. And all week Trey's heart sang.

Here come the Mighty Klutzes!

He'd like to see a scientist try to explain that.

CHAPTER 16

Home

"**D**id you see the tournament schedule?" Spider passed a blue sheet of paper to Trey. The boys huddled together in the bustling hallway outside the gym doors. It was Saturday morning, but there were people all over the place. Kids in gym shorts, parents with cameras and cell phones, and the echoing *boing, boing, boing* of basketballs bouncing on the tiled hallways and hardwood gym floor.

Spider tried not to gape at Trey, but it wasn't easy, since Trey was standing about two feet away. Trey had somehow acquired two new lime-colored wristbands, which he now wore on each of his wrists. His shorts were Very Short and Extremely Bright Orange and his long, thin legs were hairless as eggs. He wore black socks. The word GEEK, in neon letters, flashed across Spider's mind. But he pushed the thought aside. It was, after all, just Trey being Trey. Maybe later Spider could explain to him how basketball clothing had changed over the past thirty years, and that it was Maybe Not So Cool to look like he just walked in from a 1970s Dork Convention. Instead, Spider said, "It looks like we play you guys in the third round today."

"Oh," Trey answered.

Spider didn't know what else to say. He had hoped to avoid playing Trey and Ava's team. It would be an easy win, but there wouldn't be any fun in it. He'd rather kick a dead cat.

At that moment, Ms. Lobel turned down the hallway. She wore high-top sneakers, powder-blue Duke basketball shorts, and a sleeveless Nike T-shirt, revealing surprisingly muscular arms. "Good morning, Trey, Spider. You boys up for a little ball?"

Spider looked from Ms. Lobel to Trey. His eyes widened. "Is she…?"

"Yep," Trey answered proudly. "Ms. Lobel is a Mighty Klutz."

Oh, boy, what a team. Trey, Ava, and the school librarian. Spider shook his head. Hopefully it would end quickly, without anyone poking out an eye or having his library card revoked.

Spider glimpsed Kurt and Ryan as they entered the building from the side doors. "So, um, I gotta go. Good luck, okay?" Spider said to Trey.

"Okeydoke, artichokie," Trey answered.

Spider grinned. He had to admit it. Weird or not, Trey cracked him up. He hustled over to join Kurt and Ryan, who greeted him with a complicated series of fist-taps, chest thumps, and war whoops.

The first part of the morning was all about "skill stations." Groups of kids moved to different areas, where boys and girls from the varsity teams instructed them in a variety of basketball skills: dribbling, passing, foul shooting, lay-ups, that kind of stuff. It was pretty cool, but for the fourth and fifth graders it was just a warm-up for the main event: the three-on-three tournament.

There were more teams in the tournament than available court space, so Spider and his teammates had plenty of breaks to check out the action. They sat together high in the stands.

"Dude, check out what Trey Cooper is wearing," Ryan chortled. "You think those shorts are short enough?"

Kurt nodded, but seemed more intent on studying the competition. "Jasper's team looks tough," he said, pointing out a group of likely rivals to Spider.

Ryan paid them no attention. He remained focused on Trey. "Is he really playing with Ava *and* the school librarian? They are going to get crushed!" Ryan laughed mirthlessly. "Just look at those guys."

"I *am* looking," Spider finally said, an edge to his voice. "It sure looks like they're having fun to me."

That shut Ryan up. For a minute, anyway. But like Ryan, Spider couldn't help but watch the Mighty Klutzes as they got clobbered by another team. Ms. Lobel was surprisingly quick and athletic, but she didn't shoot much. Ava looked cute in a ponytail and T-shirt, but whatever she was playing, it sure wasn't basketball. And Trey, well, was Trey.

But still.

They were laughing and smiling, high-fiving and enjoying themselves. There was a part of Spider that wanted to climb down to the court and join them. It surprised Spider to feel that way. Even though he and Ryan were looking at the same thing—those clumsy Mighty Klutzes—they saw it through completely different eyes.

Finally, inevitably, it came time for Spider's team to face off against Trey's team. The game started with nods and handshakes. The atmosphere in the crowded gym was loose and upbeat. Parents and friends were watching from the stands, but at the same time, nobody really cared who won. Except for Ryan Donovan, who always cared and always kept score.

After a few easy shots, Ryan bulled his way over Trey to score a lay-up. A steamroller would have had a tougher time flattening a cupcake. Spider's team led 4–0 (counting by ones). The slaughter was on.

"Just for fun!"

"Hip-hip-hooray!"

"It's all for a good cause!"

Yeah, right.

Ms. Lobel stopped smiling. "Okaaaaay," she told Ava and Trey, loud enough for Spider to hear. "So that's the way they want it. Let's show them what we're all about."

"Sure, Ms. Lobel," Trey said, gently probing his tender elbow. "But what *are* we all about?"

A change had come over Ms. Lobel. The

librarian's eyes narrowed, ablaze. She glanced toward Spider, Ryan, and Kurt. "We're going old school, Trey."

And at that moment, the sweet and friendly librarian, Ms. Hildreth Lobel, turned into a One-Woman Wrecking Crew.

Bang, bang, bang. Ms. Lobel fired up three straight shots from downtown. Nothing but net each time. Then she went to work inside, spinning, driving, slashing to the hoop, making one basket after another. There was nothing Spider and his teammates could do to stop her.

"Wow," Ryan said in disbelief after Ms. Lobel sank a reverse lay-up. "You're awesome...for a librarian and everything."

That seemed to snap Ms. Lobel out of it. She laughed at Ryan's comment, like she laughed at most things. Besides, she had made her point. Ahead by a score of 7–5, Ms. Lobel eased up. She stopped taking shots. Instead, she focused on passing. She hit Trey with a behind-the-back pass; he let it bounce off his hands. Ava flung up a couple of air balls. Trey had a shot blocked by Kurt. Spider's team led, 9–8, when time ran out and the final whistle blew.

Trey and Ava didn't seem to mind. The important thing, they agreed, was that Spiro Agnew Elementary raised $22,478 and donated it all to the American Heart Association.

At the end of the day, Spider split off from Kurt and Ryan. They had lost to Jasper's team in their final game, but they mostly just ran out of gas. And there was no doubt about it. Ryan was an amazing player…and kind of a goon. Spider liked Kurt, though, and could sense that they were becoming good friends.

"Catch you later," Spider told Kurt. "I'm beat."

"Yeah, I know what you mean," Kurt said, wiping the sweat from his forehead. "Have a good one. I'll see you at Billy's house tonight, right?"

Spider nodded. "Yeah, I'll be there."

He found Ava and Trey as they gathered their things. "You guys played really well," he said.

"Really?" Trey asked.

Spider grinned. "Well, no, not really. You still kind of suck."

Trey laughed. After all, it was totally true and it didn't matter.

Ava said she had to go. "Thanks, Trey. I had a great time."

"Me, too."

"My parents are driving. Do you guys need a ride?" she offered.

"Nah, we'll walk home," Spider said. "It's just a couple of blocks." He glanced at Trey. "I mean, if that's all right with you, Trey?"

Trey looked up, his eyes not quite meeting Spider's. He slipped his backpack on and started walking. Maybe it was the way Trey held his shoulders, turned slightly open to Spider, or how his pace slowed to wait for his friend, but Spider understood that Trey had said yes in his own way.

The boys walked down Maple Street. They avoided the sidewalk and took the edge of the road. The sky had gone gray. Darkness began to fall like a curtain. The leaves had nearly all let go their grip; the tree branches were mostly bare. A long winter was on its way.

The boys didn't talk. But it wasn't an awkward silence. It was just the familiar quiet of many days spent together, of times when friends don't need words. Everything was okay. Trey was Trey, and Spider was Spider. They didn't know about the future, or where it would take them, but nobody ever does.

They just walked home, together.

Trey didn't stop when they arrived at the edge of his yard. Without a word, he cut across the grass, heading to the front door in a precise diagonal. No good-bye, no see ya later.

Spider watched his friend head for the door. Trey walked flat-footed, his head bent slightly forward, eyes on the ground.

"I'll see you tomorrow," Spider called out.

Trey didn't answer. Maybe he didn't hear. But

for a moment, just a fraction of time, he held the door suspended in his grip. Without looking back, Trey nodded, yes, tomorrow, then stepped inside, yes, and was gone.

ACKNOWLEDGEMENTS

In writing this book, I relied on the help and inspiration of Chris Porter, a fifth-grade teacher at Glenmont Elementary in upstate New York. Chris invited me into her classroom, where I was free to visit almost any time throughout the school year. She never asked what I was doing, or what I was writing — which was a good thing, because for a long time I had no idea. My goal was simply to sit and absorb the goings-on of a lively, happy, creative fifth-grade classroom. I'd say that Chris provided that effortlessly, if not for how hard and long she worked.

I am grateful to the boys and girls of that 2006–07 class, for having the good sense to pretend I was invisible, even when trespassing on their turf. None of them are depicted in this book in any way whatsoever, but each helped ground this story in something close, I hope, to reality.

Many individuals at Glenmont — from teachers to noon aides to social workers — spoke with me and shared insight. This isn't the Oscars, so I'll refrain from a lengthy list. But they do have my thanks, most especially Principal Laura Heffernan.

After speaking with and observing a librarian, Julia Healy, at Lynnwood Elementary, I came up with the basis for this book's Ms. Lobel. Before I met Julia, there was no librarian in the story. Five minutes later, there had to be.

Somewhere along the line the themes in this book began to take hold. When responding to an email query, Chris Porter wrote to me, *"I know as a fifth grade teacher, I always hope that the 'troubled' student who doesn't fit in the mainstream group is able to find just one friend. I truly believe you can get through anything knowing that you have someone who likes you and sees you for just you — as well as someone who will include you in the most difficult times of the day — recess/lunch!"*

I taped those words to my wall.

I was similarly inspired in my reading about

Spectrum Disorders. This research helped inform the character of Trey Cooper. While I came across many fine books, articles, and websites, one book in particular merits special mention: *Elijah's Cup*, by Valerie Paradiz. It is the perceptive, honest, heartfelt, illuminating story of a mother struggling to raise an autistic child. It blew me away. In addition, the work of Temple Grandin stands out as remarkably frank and inspiring. This is a list that could go on for a while — so many great books are being written — so I'll stop here.

I am grateful to my editor, Shannon Penney, for her intelligence and dedication.

I mean to say: I've been blessed with wonderful resources and helping hands. But any shortcomings in this book can be traced back to the author.

Lastly, thanks to my family, Lisa, Nick, Gavin, and Maggie.